Remy Marland o b
God of Driver's da
today. Remy's fin
torn, pale blue jean.
sirable piece of laminate   , of
course, was her future driver's license.)

Next to her, Christine prayed not to drive today or ever.
Poor Christine held her shiny name tag in her lap, ready
for Remy to snatch up.

"All right, class," said Mr. Fielding. He didn't look at
them, because he never looked at them. He looked only at
his enrollment book. "Remy, Christine, and Morgan will
drive with me today."

"Yes!" yelled Remy. She didn't have to exchange a name
tag after all. She jumped up so fast, she knocked her books
on the floor, tried to grab them, and tripped over Taft's
extended legs.

This was not clumsiness. It was calculated. Remy was
the Distraction Princess, because even Mr. Fielding might
one day catch on to what was happening.